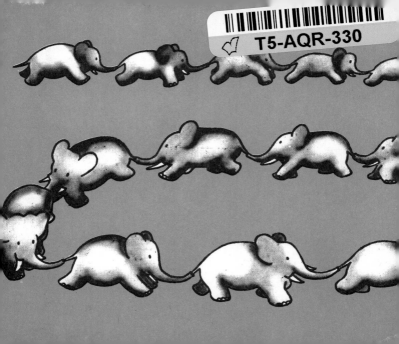

BABAR
at the
Seashore

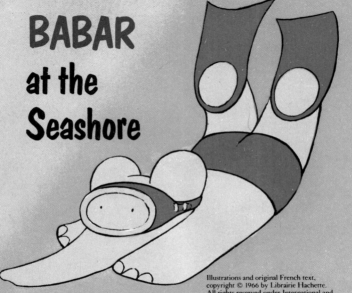

by Laurent de Brunhoff

Translated by Merle S. Haas

Babar and Celeste are at the seashore.

Celeste loves to sun-bathe.

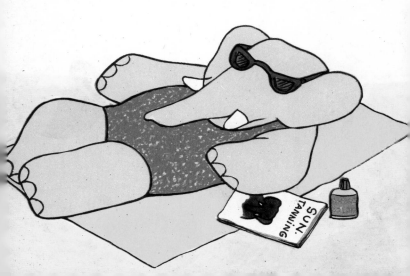

Pom and Alexander are playing football.
Arthur and Flora run to join them.

Digging for crabs at low tide.
My, what fun!

It is also great fun to build a sand castle, decorate it with seashells, and then wait to watch the waves roll in and wash it all away.

The sand castle has been swept away.
The sea carried it away. Celeste and the three
children are playing ball in the surf.

Flora and Alexander steal up quietly and upset the air mattress. Arthur tumbles off into the water!

Babar organizes a boat ride.

They anchor in a lovely bay. Arthur dives into the water. Pom, Flora and Alexander are all set for an underwater expedition.

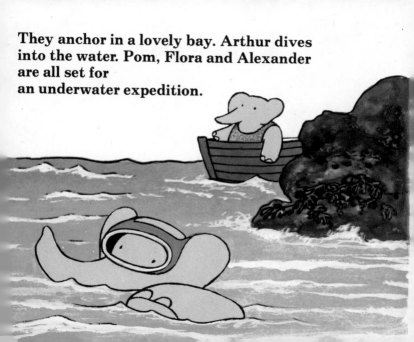

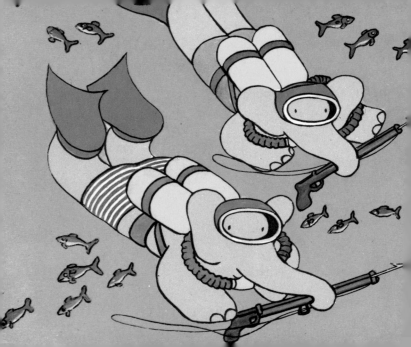

Alexander
aims at
an enormous
fish…

Alexander has caught the big fish.
Pom and Flora help him bring it in!

Bravo, Alexander!
Bravo, Flora!
Bravo, Pom!

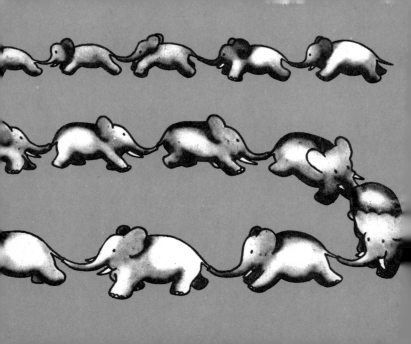